A CAST IS THE

Perfect Accessory

(AND OTHER LESSONS I'VE LEARNED)

DON'T MISS THE FIRST BOOK
OF MANDY BERR'S ADVENTURES!

DON'T WEAR

Polka-Dot Underwear

WITH WHITE PANTS
(AND OTHER LESSONS I'VE LEARNED)

A CAST IS THE

Perfect Accessory

(AND OTHER LESSONS I'VE LEARNED)

BY ALLISON GUTKNECHT

ILLUSTRATED BY STEVIE LEWIS

ALADDIN

NEW YORK   LONDON   TORONTO   SYDNEY   NEW DELHI

ALADDIN

An imprint of Simon & Schuster Children's Publishing Division
1230 Avenue of the Americas, New York, NY 10020
First Aladdin paperback edition March 2014
Text copyright © 2014 by Allison Gutknecht
Illustrations copyright © 2014 by Stevie Lewis
All rights reserved, including the right of reproduction in whole or
in part in any form.
ALADDIN is a trademark of Simon & Schuster, Inc., and related logo is a
registered trademark of Simon & Schuster, Inc.
Also available in an Aladdin hardcover edition.
For information about special discounts for bulk purchases, please contact Simon &
Schuster Special Sales at 1-866-506-1949 or business@simonandschuster.com.
The Simon & Schuster Speakers Bureau can bring authors to your live event. For
more information or to book an event, contact the Simon & Schuster Speakers
Bureau at 1-866-248-3049 or visit our website at www.simonspeakers.com.
Cover designed by Jessica Handelman
The text of this book was set in Arno Pro.
The illustrations for this book were rendered digitally.
Manufactured in the United States of America 0114 OFF
2 4 6 8 10 9 7 5 3 1
Library of Congress Control Number 2013955121
ISBN 978-1-4424-8395-8 (pbk)
ISBN 978-1-4424-8396-5 (hc)
ISBN 978-1-4424-8397-2 (eBook)

For Babci,

WHO UNDERSTOOD THE VALUE OF
WISHING OVER PENNIES

Special Thanks to

ALYSON HELLER FOR HER LIMITLESS ENTHUSIASM
AND BUSHELS OF FANCY-DANCY IDEAS,
AND TO CHARLIE OLSEN FOR HIS CONTINUAL
SUPPORT AND GUIDANCE OF BOTH MANDY
AND ME. ENDLESS APPRECIATION TO
THE TEAMS AT ALADDIN AND INKWELL FOR
HELPING TO PERFECT THE POLKA DOTS.

Contents

CHAPTER 1

The Pizza Problem

THE CENTER OF OUR PIZZA PIE IS MISSING because Dad is no good at giving directions.

The best part of a pizza slice is the first bite because the point is skinny and it is mouth-size and it never has any crust. Crust is useless because it has no cheese. I always try to make my brother Timmy eat my crust so that he will give me his first bite points. Mom says this is not allowed, but Dad does not because he is no good at giving directions.

Dad is also not a very good babysitter, if I am being honest. If he were, he would have said, *Mandy, do not touch the pizza until I come back.* Instead, Dad left me alone in the kitchen with the big, steamy pizza pie box, and he ran off to the twins' room.

One of the twins had started crying, because the twins are always crying, and I knew waiting for Dad to give me a slice could take all night. So I opened the pizza box, lifted the slices one by one, and bit off each delicious point before plopping the rest of the slice back in the box.

It was the best pizza pie I have ever had.

Only Dad does not think so, because when he comes back into the kitchen with a crying twin and sees the center of the pizza missing, his face turns as red as a tomato. He looks over at me slowly, so I cross my arms and stomp my foot and yell, "I had no dinner!" before he can say one word.

Dad turns away from me, digs through the twins' diaper bag, and walks back toward the twins' room with a package of wipes in his hand.

"Follow me," he calls over his shoulder. I keep my arms crossed and drag my heels on the kitchen floor.

"I had no dinner!" I repeat when we get to the twins' doorway.

"You need to learn to be patient, Mandy," Dad says. "Even Timmy did not take bites out of all of the pizza slices, and he's only three. You're eight—you should know better." And this makes me angry because I know I am better than Timmy, which is why Timmy is hungry right now and I am not.

"You are a bad babysitter," I inform Dad. "I am going to tell Mom on you." Dad laughs then, which I think is rude.

"And what are you going to tell her?" Dad asks.

He begins changing the diaper of one of the twins, which is smelly and awful, so I hold my nose shut.

"Yow dow nawt ghive guwd dewektons," I answer.

"What?"

"Yow dow nawt ghive guwd dewektons," I repeat.

"I can't understand you when you're holding your nose," Dad says.

I whip my hand away from my face and yell, "YOU DO NOT GIVE GOOD DIRECTIONS!" real fast, and I guess I say it pretty loud, because the twin starts to cry again.

"Mandy," Dad begins in his "This is your warning" voice. "I think you should come here and help me change Samantha's diaper."

"No, thank you," I answer, and I am polite and everything.

"It's not a choice, Amanda," Dad says, and

I know that he means business. Dad only calls me "Amanda" when I am about to be in trouble, because he knows that I hate it.

I sigh a big puff of breath and shuffle over to the twins' changing table. I put one hand over my nose and my other hand over the twin's mouth and say, "Stop crying," which I think is pretty helpful.

"Mandy, no!" Dad pulls my hand away from the twin. "You can't cover her mouth like that— she won't be able to breathe."

"Then what do you want me to do?" I stomp my foot again. I would like to go up to my room and be in trouble by myself, but I stay put because I do not want to make Dad call me "Amanda" again.

"Here." Dad fastens the twin's new diaper and picks her up under the armpits. "Play with Samantha until I finish changing Cody. See if you can get her to stop crying."

I stare at Dad over the hand that is still covering my nose. I never, ever hold the twins because they are damp and gross and no fun at all. Dad looks back at me, neither of us moving, and the twin continues to howl.

"Amanda," Dad says, "either you play with Samantha right now or no Rainbow Sparkle TV show for—"

"Fine." I whip my hand away from my nose and reach out for the twin, because I am not having Rainbow Sparkle taken away from me again. No way! I wrap my arms around the twin like she is a pile of dirty clothes, and I sit on the floor.

"Here is a deal," I say to her. "You will stop crying right now, and I will tell you the secret about pizza." I lay the twin on the floor because I do not like damp things in my hands, and she almost starts being quiet.

"See? Your sister likes when you talk to her," Dad says as he spreads the other twin out on the changing table. But I do not answer him because I do not care what the twins like.

"The secret about pizza is that the points are the best part. The crust is the worst, because there is no cheese, but the best part is the first bite of a slice. And also, the best color in the whole world is periwinkle." I look up at Dad. "Am I done?" The twin is not crying anymore, so it only seems fair.

"No, now play with Cody while I—"

"Anybody home?" Mom calls from the living room. I dart out of the twins' room and run to her so I can tattle on Dad. She and Grandmom are piling shopping bags on our couch.

"Abracadabra!" Timmy runs down the stairs and leaps over the last three steps, landing with a thud next to the front door.

"Timmy!" Mom yells as he picks himself up. "What did I tell you about jumping off the stairs? You're going to break a bone."

"Sorry," Timmy answers, and he tries to climb Grandmom like a jungle gym until she scoops him into her arms. He gives her a slobbery kiss.

"Yuck," I call.

"Hi, Mandy," Grandmom greets me as Timmy slinks down her body like a snake.

"Did you get me gummy bears?" I ask. Grandmoms are the best people for giving gummy bears because moms and dads usually say no.

"Not even a hello first?" Grandmom asks. "Come give me some sugar." Grandmom says to "give her sugar" when she wants a kiss, which is pretty silly, I think. Even if I am the sweetest person in my family, I would be sweeter if I had gummy bears first.

I kiss Grandmom on the lips, and I am not as

slobbery as Timmy about it. "How about those bears?" I ask again.

"Not today," Grandmom says. "Maybe next time." But next time is not helpful at all when I want gummy bears now.

"Well, how about my fancy-dancy periwinkle sunglasses?" I ask. I have wanted fancy-dancy periwinkle sunglasses for my whole entire life and still do not have any, so every time Mom and Grandmom go shopping, I ask them to buy me a pair.

"Mandy," Mom says, "no more B-R-A-T behavior, please."

"Why are we spelling?" Grandmom whispers to Mom, like she thinks I cannot hear anything.

"Because Timmy is a brat," I answer.

"Brat!" Timmy repeats, and he looks pretty proud of himself.

Mom rolls her eyes up to the ceiling and looks

at Grandmom. "That's why." She points to Timmy. "And, Mandy, don't call your brother a B-R-A-T."

"But—" I begin, but Mom interrupts me because she is never a good listener about my problems.

"Help me carry these bags of change into the laundry room, please," she says, picking up a pillowcase, which clinks and clanks as she swings it back and forth.

"Why do you have bags of change?" I ask.

"Your mom's taking them to the bank to put them in the magic coin machine for me," Grand-mom explains. "It will turn the coins into dollar bills."

"It's magic?" Timmy asks excitedly.

"No, stupid," I say, even though I am not completely sure.

"Mandy!" Mom yells from the laundry room. "No S-T-U-P-I-D talk either."

··· ‖ ···

"When you get the dollars, are you going to buy me my fancy-dancy periwinkle sunglasses?" I ask Grandmom.

"We'll see," Grandmom answers, which means "no" in grown-up talk. "I think you would enjoy those sunglasses even more if you bought them yourself. Don't you think?"

"I have no dollars," I answer, because that is the truth.

"You get an allowance, don't you?"

"Yes, but that is only two quarters," I explain. "No dollars."

"Then save up your quarters until you can take them to the magic coin machine and exchange them for dollars," Grandmom suggests. "When you have enough, you can buy the fancy-dancy sunglasses yourself."

"Periwinkle," I add.

"What?"

"You forgot 'periwinkle.' They are fancy-dancy *periwinkle* sunglasses," I explain.

"Right," Grandmom answers, and she pats me on the head like I am a dog. "Now come help your mother with these bags."

I sling a pillowcase over my shoulder, and it is very heavy. I lug it slowly to the laundry room.

"Right there on the floor, next to the others," Mom instructs, pointing. I dump the pillowcase on the floor with a crash, and this noise makes the twins start crying again.

"Mandy, be careful!" Mom calls from the kitchen, and I stick my tongue out because she is not here to see. I hear Grandmom and Dad in the twins' room trying to make them stop crying, so I sit on the floor of the laundry room because I do not want to talk to the twins again. I place my hands in one of the pillowcases and lift a humon-gous handful of coins in the air. I release them and let them sprinkle back into the pile, tinkling like raindrops.

There must be thousands and millions of coins in these bags—more than enough to buy my fancy-dancy periwinkle sunglasses.

"Tim, what happened to this pizza?" I hear Mom yell from the kitchen, and then I remember that I forgot to tell on Dad for being no good at giving directions.

"Ask Mandy," Dad calls back, so I leap to my feet real fast to close the laundry room door. I do not feel like talking about pizza points right now. Not when I have to figure out how to col-lect enough coins to buy my very own pair of fancy-dancy periwinkle sunglasses.

And maybe my own pizza, too.

CHAPTER 2

Buddy Blues

MRS. SPANGLE IS MUCH BETTER AT GIVING directions than Dad, but she is best at making up classroom rules. We have a list of eight rules hanging next to the board, and I think that is way too many. Mrs. Spangle's newest rule is "No rocking on two chair legs," and it is not one of my favorites.

Sometimes it is necessary to rock my chair back on two legs because it is the only way I can talk to Anya. Anya is my favorite person in the world, at least most of the time, but her desk is behind me, so she is very hard to reach. I told Mrs. Spangle that I would not need to rock my chair back on two legs if she would just let Anya sit next to me, but she said, "Absolutely not."

Instead, I have to sit next to Natalie all marking period. Natalie is not as boring as she used to be, but she is still not very fun, either. Natalie never rocks her chair on two legs or calls out or breaks any of Mrs. Spangle's rules.

Luckily, though, Natalie is missing from school today, so I have a lot of room to spread out my things.

"Psst," I whisper to Anya, but she does not answer. I look over my shoulder to make sure Mrs. Spangle is not watching, then I lean my chair back on two legs so I can reach Anya's shoulder. "Psst, Anya." I pull gently on the end of one of her wispy blond curls.

"What?" Anya is busy with her seatwork

because she is not as fast as me. Mrs. Spangle says that if we finish our seatwork early, we should do some silent reading at our desk. But I am always finished early, so I get very tired of being quiet.

"Natalie's missing," I tell her.

"She's probably sick," Anya guesses, but she keeps working on her seatwork instead of paying good attention to me, which I think is rude.

"Maybe she's getting new glasses," I whisper. "Maybe she'll get a better color than those dull black—"

"Mandy!" Mrs. Spangle's voice startles me, and the front two legs of my chair fall back on the ground with a crash. Her red porcupine hair is wild as she whips her hand toward the CLASSROOM RULES sign and points to number eight.

"What does this say?" she asks. But I do not answer because Mrs. Spangle already knows that I am an excellent reader.

"We're waiting, Mandy," she continues. "Remind us all of our new classroom rule, please." I pinch my mouth together and do not say one word.

"Mandy . . ." Mrs. Spangle says my name slowly. "I'm going to count to three before you lose recess for the day. One . . ."

But before Mrs. Spangle can count any higher,

our classroom door opens, and Natalie walks in with the school nurse behind her.

And Natalie is not boring at all right now because her right arm is wrapped in a cast. A cast! A real-life cast! I have always wanted to wear a cast—a pretty periwinkle one that I could draw pictures of Rainbow Sparkle all over. But Mom says I can only get one if I break a bone, and I am not very clumsy, I think.

"What happened to your arm?" Dennis calls out to Natalie, and Mrs. Spangle does not even yell at him for breaking rule number four.

"I broke my wrist," Natalie answers, and she sounds pretty sad about it actually. And this is ridiculous, because if I broke my wrist, I would be the happiest I have ever been in my life. I would use a sling with glitter all over it so that everyone would know right away that I had a cast, and they would ask me how I broke a bone. And then I would get to tell them a fantastic story about what happened, which is really the best part of having a cast.

"When did you break it?"

"Does it hurt?"

"How long do you have to wear the cast?"

My class calls out questions to Natalie one right after another, and Mrs. Spangle does not even say anything about them not raising their hands (but she also forgets to give me a warning about the chair legs, so this is not a total tragedy).

"That's enough, everyone," Mrs. Spangle says. "Natalie, let's get you a classroom buddy to help you get settled, okay?" Natalie nods her head shyly and looks down at her cast. And I slouch way down in my seat so that Mrs. Spangle can't see me, because I am absolutely positive that I do not want to be Natalie's buddy. Natalie is very bossy, and she will think she is in charge of me, and I always like to be the one in charge.

Mrs. Spangle glances across the room to Natalie's desk, and I slide so far down in my chair that my bottom almost falls off it.

"Mandy"—Mrs. Spangle's eyes land on me anyway—"since you sit right next to Natalie, how about if you be her buddy for the week?" And I know that even though Mrs. Spangle is asking me a question, I am not allowed to say no, because she says it in her "I'm not asking, I'm telling" voice.

I look from Mrs. Spangle to Natalie and back again, and I do not say one word.

"Ahem." Mrs. Spangle clears her throat at me. "Let's get a move on, Mandy. Help Natalie put away her book bag, please."

I sigh very loudly then, but I pull myself up from my slouch and walk over to Natalie. I take her book bag from the nurse's hands, and we walk to the cubbies.

"Take out my homework folder," Natalie whispers.

"Please," I remind her, because that is one of Mrs. Spangle's rules that I am good at: "Be polite."

"Please," Natalie says. "And put my lunch box on the top shelf."

I give Natalie my "You are driving me bananas" face and tap my toe against the ground, waiting.

"Please," Natalie finally adds. So I pull her lunch box out of her bag and hand it to her.

"You can put it on the shelf yourself," I tell her. "You have one perfectly good arm."

"Can you please just do it for me?" Natalie asks. "I'm sore." So I squint my eyes at her and throw her lunch box onto the top shelf of her cubby.

"How did you break your wrist?" I ask.

"I don't want to talk about it," Natalie responds, which is not a good answer.

I drop her book bag on the ground and cross my arms. "Tell me," I demand. "I will not tell anyone else. I pinky swear." But I do not hold out my pinky to shake with Natalie, because I might have to tell Anya the story. Plus, Natalie's good pinky is covered by the cast.

Natalie shakes her head. "I don't want to talk about it," she repeats.

"But if I am your buddy, then I should get to know the—"

"Mandy, Natalie, let's go," Mrs. Spangle calls, interrupting me. I take out Natalie's homework folder, shove the bag into her cubby, and hand the folder over to her roughly.

"You can carry this yourself," I say, and I return to my seat in a huff and a puff. Natalie follows me, and when she cannot pull out her chair herself, Mrs. Spangle makes me do it for her.

The minute she sits down, Natalie says,

"Mandy, take your stuff off my desk," so I roll my eyes all the way up to the ceiling and slide my pencil box and markers and seatwork and silent reading book back onto my own desktop. "And rip the seatwork page out of my math workbook for me. And get me a pencil out of my case."

"PLEASE," I say, pointing to our CLASSROOM RULES sign. "It is number six on the list: Be polite!"

"Mandy!" Mrs. Spangle yells. "That's a warning." She walks over to the board and places a big *M.B.* on the initials list.

"Oooh, Polka Dot's in trouble," Dennis says in a singsong voice. Dennis has called me "Polka Dot" ever since he found out I wear polka-dot underwear sometimes, but I call him "Freckle Face" right back because his nose is covered with freckles. Even though, to tell you the truth,

I would kind of like to have some freckles myself.

I whip my head around just in time to see Anya kick Dennis under his desk, which is why Anya is my friend and Dennis is not.

"Thank you," I whisper to Anya, and then I turn back to Natalie.

"I liked it better when you were absent," I say to her, and I slide my hands across my desk, spreading my things back across both of our desktops.

And Natalie cannot do anything about it, because she doesn't know how to say "please."

It is very hard to have a good day when you need to be somebody's buddy and you do not want to be. Mom does not understand this because when she asks, "How was school?" and I answer, "I had to help Natalie all day because she broke her wrist," she replies, "Oh no, is Natalie okay?"

What Mom should have said is, *Oh no, it must have been terrible being Natalie's buddy!* But Mom does not understand real problems.

"She will not even tell anyone how she broke it," I complain. Mom is holding a twin, and he is whimpering like he might start howling at any second.

"Maybe she doesn't want everybody to know," Mom guesses, and she switches the twin from one hip to the other.

"Oh please," I say. "The best part of breaking a bone is telling the story about how you did it. Everyone knows that."

"Well, maybe Natalie's embarrassed," Mom says. "Maybe she broke it in a way she doesn't want everybody to know about."

And I hate to say it after I made the big deal with the "Oh please" and all, but this is a pretty interesting idea.

"Like what?" I ask.

"Like she fell riding her bike," Mom says.

"That is not embarrassing."

"Or she fell roller-skating," Mom says.

"That is not embarrassing."

"Or she fell down the stairs," Mom says.

"That is not embarrassing."

Mom spreads her lips into a thin line and gives me her "You are getting on my nerves" face. "Mandy, just because you don't think something is embarrassing doesn't mean that Natalie won't," she tells me. "I bet Natalie thinks a lot more things are embarrassing than you do."

I think about this for one moment. Maybe Mom is right about what Natalie thinks is an embarrassing story. I will ask her tomorrow, and if she broke her wrist in any of the ways that Mom guessed, I will tell her that—ta-da!—that is not something to be embarrassed about. And also, I will tell her how to make her story more interesting, because the story is the best part of having a broken bone.

"So when Dad gets home, I'm going to the bank to exchange Grandmom's coins. Do you want to come with me?" Mom asks.

"Are the twins going?"

"No," Mom answers.

"Is Timmy going?"

"Yes," she says.

"I do not want to go if Timmy is going," I say.

"Fine, then you can stay here with Dad and the twins."

"No!" I respond. "Dad is a bad babysitter, you know."

"Then come to the bank with us," Mom says. "I know you want to see that magic coin machine in action." But I only want to see the magic coin machine if I can put my own coins into it and get some dollars out.

"Will you let me put in the coins myself?" I ask.

"Yes, you and Timmy can do it together," Mom answers. "Now, if you're going to go, get started on your homework." She waves her hand toward my book bag just as the twin starts wailing.

I cover my ears and yell, "I will do it upstairs!" I grab my book bag from the couch and bang up the steps and into my room. But I do not work on my homework because I have something much more important to do first: find some change. I cannot go all the way to the magic coin machine and come away with no dollars to use toward my fancy-dancy periwinkle sunglasses.

I rattle the piggy bank where I am supposed to keep my allowance, but it is empty since I used all of my money to buy ten balls of gum, just to see if I could chew it at once. I crawl along the floor of my room slowly, looking for any lost change, but I find only a cheese puff, a button, and an old tooth-breaker gummy bear (I know it is a tooth-breaker because I stick it in my mouth and it almost breaks my teeth).

Very quietly, I head downstairs to check under the couch cushions. Luckily, the twin is still howling, so Mom cannot hear what I'm doing. I stick my hand in between two of the cushions and then two more, and I find a dime. A dime! Ten whole cents. It is not much, I guess, but it is better than nothing.

"What you doing, Mandy?" Timmy startles me so much that I almost fall off the couch and hit my head.

"You almost made me egg my head open," I tell him. Mom always tells me not to crack my head open, but I think eggs are the best things to crack, so I say "egg my head open."

"What you doing, Mandy?" Timmy repeats.

"None of your beeswax," I answer. I cannot have Timmy looking for lost change too. No way! I am not splitting my money with a preschooler. Not when there are fancy-dancy periwinkle sunglasses to be bought.

"I am going back upstairs," I tell him. "Don't follow me." I scurry up the stairs and into Mom and Dad's bedroom. I clutch my one dime between my fingers and crawl around the floor. The best part about Mom and Dad's bedroom is the window because it is huge and it is wide and it faces the front yard. I have only one small window in my room and it faces a tree, so that is not useful at all. I stand in Mom and Dad's window and look outside. Our neighborhood is all out in front of me, and it is a very good spot for being nosy. I look from one neighbor's house to the next, and I try to see into their windows. A car drives down the street, and then I see it: Right in the middle of our road is a sparkly, shiny, golden circle. A coin! It has to be a coin. And I have to get it immediately.

Only I am not allowed in the street without a grown-up watching. Not ever. Not even if I look both ways and everything.

I stick my head down the top of the stairs and listen to make sure a twin is still howling. Then I tiptoe down the first six steps to see if Timmy is in the living room, and I shimmy down the rest when I see that he is not. Fast as a flash, I open the front door and run across our yard. I reach the curb, look both ways, and dart into the street.

And I cannot find the coin anywhere.

I walk back and forth on the pavement looking down, and when that doesn't work, I bend my knees to look closer.

"AMANDA IRENE BERR! GET OUT OF THE STREET THIS INSTANT!" I look up to see Mom running through our front yard, a twin flapping on her hip. Before I have a chance to stand, she yanks me up by my armpit and pulls me onto the sidewalk. Timmy watches us from the open front door, and I stick my tongue out at him for being a snoop.

"What were you doing?" Mom asks in her angriest voice.

"Looking for a coin," I answer.

"What is the rule about the street?"

"Don't go in the street without a grown-up watching," I answer.

"Well?"

I shrug. "I looked both ways," I tell her.

"Room. Now." Mom points me inside. "And no bank for you later. Absolutely not."

I stomp up the stairs and slam the door to my room. I flop onto my bed and hold my chin in my hands, and that's when it hits me: Not only did I not find the coin in the street, but now I lost my dime somewhere too.

And with this kind of coin luck, I am never going to be able to buy my own fancy-dancy periwinkle sunglasses. And this is the most gigantic tragedy of all.

CHAPTER 3

Becoming Famous

MRS. SPANGLE ASKED ME TO HELP NATALIE take her pencil case out of her desk, and I said, "Only if she gives me a quarter," and now my initials are on the board again. I do not think this is fair because I am tired of being Natalie's buddy, and plus, I need some coins if I am ever going to get my fancy-dancy periwinkle sunglasses.

Mom made me stay in my room all of last night except for dinner, which was not even worth it because it was pork chops, and I hate pork chops.

And then she took Timmy with her to the bank to use the magic coin machine, and I got to do nothing. Plus, I never even found the dime I had lost, so now I am back to having no coins at all, and this week is turning out not so hot.

I pull Natalie's stupid pencil case out of her desk for her, and she does not even thank me. I plop it down so that it makes a loud noise, and Mrs. Spangle tells me to "Knock it off," so I do, but only because I do not want to miss recess.

"Psst," I whisper to Natalie. "Did you fall off your bike?"

"Huh?"

"Did you fall off your bike? Is that how you broke your wrist?"

"No," Natalie answers.

"Did you fall roller-skating?" I ask.

"No."

"Did you fall down the stairs?"

"No, Mandy," Natalie answers, like I am a dope or something. "I don't want to talk about it."

"Well, that is ridiculous," I tell her. "The best part of breaking a bone is telling the story of how you did it. Everybody knows that." But Natalie just looks down at her cast through her glasses and doesn't answer me. "And also, your cast is a boring color." If I were lucky enough to have a cast, I would pick a stand-out-and-shout color, but Natalie's cast is white. And I hate white things.

"Open to the next clean page of your writing journals, please," Mrs. Spangle tells us. "I'd like you to write a five-sentence summary of the last story you read in your reading group. Who can remind us what a summary is?"

Natalie shoots her good hand in the air.

"Yes, Natalie?" Mrs. Spangle calls on her.

"The main idea of what happened in the story,

with some details," Natalie answers, and she looks pretty proud of herself.

"Excellent answer," Mrs. Spangle tells her, and I cross my arms because I did not think it was so great. "Natalie, are you going to be okay writing with your left hand again?" Natalie broke her right wrist, and because she is right-handed, she has to use her left hand to write now.

"I think so," Natalie answers.

"Just try your best," Mrs. Spangle tells her. "The rest of you have fifteen minutes—remember, five sentences all together."

I uncross my arms to begin writing, and Mrs. Spangle circles the room to watch us work. When she gets to our group, she leans over Natalie's shoulder.

"You're doing a beautiful job," she tells her. "Maybe you were meant to be left-handed after all!" Natalie grins an enormous smile at her, and

I look down at her journal to see her work. Her handwriting looks pretty awful, and I am positive I could do a better job with my own left hand.

Carefully, I move my pencil from my right hand to my left, grip the whole thing in all of my fingers, place the point on the journal, and press down.

And I press a hole right through the paper.

I lift the pencil back up, rearrange my fingers so only three are on top, and try again. And this time, I draw a thick line down the entire page.

Hmm. This writing with my left hand business is harder than I thought.

I place just two fingers on top of the pencil and try once more, and now my hand is steadier. I decide that before I do anything else, I better learn to write my own name with my left hand. Slowly, I make the shape of an *M* at the top of the paper, followed by an *a* and then an *n*.

Just as I am finally getting to the curlicue of the *y*, Mrs. Spangle calls out, "Time's up. Everyone, please place your journals in the basket on my desk so I can check them during lunch. Leave them open to the page you were working on."

Uh-oh.

I look down at my journal—at the hole and the line and my wobbly name across the top. I have not written any part of the summary except the words "In the story," and I know this is going to be a problem.

"Natalie, come here for a second," Mrs. Spangle calls. "Mandy can bring up your journal for you." I watch Natalie walk to Mrs. Spangle, who whispers something in her ear. Natalie smiles and nods.

"Class," Mrs. Spangle begins, "Natalie and I think it would be a nice idea if each of you had a chance to autograph her cast. What do you think?"

My class whoops and cheers, but I do not even let out one "Wahoo." Natalie returns to her seat, and Mrs. Spangle hands her a package of colorful markers for everyone to use to sign their names.

"Mandy, can you put my journal in Mrs. Spangle's basket, please?" Natalie asks as one classmate after another comes over and writes his or her name gently across Natalie's cast.

"Only after I get to sign," I tell her. "I have to be your buddy, so I should have gotten to go first." I pick up a black marker, because Natalie is the one who chose the boring old white cast and her boring old black glasses, so she should not get to have any fancy-dancy colors. I place the marker in my left hand with two fingers on top.

"Stand back, everybody," I say. "I am going to show you how easy it is to write with your left hand." Before Natalie can let out one peep, I place the marker on the cast and try to drag my hand into an *M* shape. It is harder to write on the cast than I had thought, because it has a lot of bumps and ridges, so I have a little trouble.

Actually, I have a lot of trouble.

So much trouble that by the time I am finished signing my name, *Mandy* takes up half of Natalie's cast.

"Mandy!" Natalie screeches with so much exclaim that it does not sound like Natalie at all. She shoots her left hand in the air and waves Mrs. Spangle over. "Look what Mandy did." She points to my signature.

Mrs. Spangle looks at me out of the side of her eyes, and it is a pretty scary look, if I am being honest. Without a word, Mrs. Spangle approaches the board and places a check mark next to my initials.

"Oooh, Polka Dot's in big trouble," Dennis whispers.

"Be quiet, Dennis," Anya hisses, defending me, but I cannot even thank her because I am too busy watching Mrs. Spangle come over to our group.

"Scoot your chair back," she says to Natalie. Natalie does, and then Mrs. Spangle slides Natalie's desk across the floor.

She slides it farther and farther away from me. Wahoo!

And then she slides it right into the space next to Anya.

"Anya, I'm hoping you can be a good helper to Natalie until her wrist gets better," Mrs. Spangle says. "What do you say?"

"Okay!" Anya answers, and I try to give Anya my "How dare you?" look, but she is too busy carrying Natalie's journal up to Mrs. Spangle's desk.

"And you, Mandy," Mrs. Spangle begins. "You're going to spend recess today fixing that mess you made in your writing journal. And you're missing tomorrow's recess, too, for what you did to Natalie's cast."

I slouch in my seat and push my lips together into a pout. It was bad enough when I had to be Natalie's buddy. But for Natalie to be the most famous person in our class and to have Anya as her buddy?

I need to put a stop to this immediately.

And also, I need to learn to write with my left hand.

CHAPTER 4

Have a Nice Trip?

"GUESS WHAT?" I YELL TO MOM THE MOMENT I bang through our front door.

"What?" Timmy calls from the living room floor. He is playing with blocks because he likes dumb baby toys.

"Guess what?" I yell even louder to Mom.

"WHAT?" Timmy answers.

"I'M NOT TALKING TO YOU!" I say in my loudest voice ever, and this finally gets Mom's attention.

"What's going on in there?" Mom appears in the doorway to the living room with no twins attached to her body for once.

"Guess what?" I repeat.

"What?" Mom asks.

"Natalie is an Anya thief," I tell her, and Mom looks at me for a second like I am not making any sense.

"What do you mean, she's an Anya thief?" she asks.

"She is trying to steal Anya from me," I explain, even though I think "Anya thief" is a very clear description of her.

"How is she trying to steal her?" Mom asks.

"Mrs. Spangle made Anya be Natalie's buddy, and—"

"I thought you were Natalie's buddy," Mom interrupts.

"That did not work out," I tell her. "So now

Anya is her buddy, which is not fair at all, because Anya is *my* friend. And also, Natalie should not need so much help."

Mom crosses her arms and looks at me like she knows something I do not.

"Why didn't it work out with you being Natalie's buddy?" she asks. "I thought you and Natalie were getting along better."

I shake my head back and forth very quickly. "She did not like how I autographed her cast."

"How did you autograph it?"

"With my left hand," I explain.

"And?"

"And it was big," I say.

"What was big?"

"My name. On the cast."

"Why did you sign it so big?"

"Because Natalie is not polite," I tell her. "She thinks she is in charge, and she is not."

Mom uncrosses her arms then and puts one of her hands on her forehead. "You know, Mandy," she tells me, "you need to let other people be the boss sometimes. It can't always be you."

"I do!" I say "do" extra loud so Mom knows I mean it. "But Natalie thinks that she is the boss of everything."

Mom shakes her head slowly. "I think we're going to have to practice you letting other people be in charge," she says. "We can't have you acting like a B-R-A-T."

"A brat!" Timmy fills in, and he looks pretty proud of himself.

"We're going to start now," Mom says. "You're going to sit with Timmy, and he is going to tell you all about what he's building. What are you building, Timmy?"

"A city!" he answers.

"Great," Mom says. "You can tell Mandy all

about it." She motions for me to sit on the floor.

"But—" I begin.

"No buts," Mom says. "And no brats. Sit there and play with your brother for at least twenty minutes. Timmy, you're in charge!"

"Yay!" Timmy calls out.

"That is not even a good exclaim," I tell him. "You're supposed to say, 'Wahoo!'"

"Mandy . . . ," Mom says with a warning in her voice. "Timmy is in charge. Not you."

I slump my shoulders toward my shoes and collapse with a loud "Humph!" on the floor. Because the only person who is worse at being in charge than Natalie is Timmy.

The next morning I wake up with the perfect plan to stop Natalie from thinking she is the boss of everybody. I am so excited about it that I leap out of bed even before Mom comes in to wake me.

I am going to create my own sling for my arm, so that I cannot use it all day in school and Mrs. Spangle will have to make Anya my buddy. It does not matter that my wrist is not really broken, because as long as it looks like it is hurt, Mrs. Spangle will be tricked. I am a genius.

I scurry under my bed and root through all of the things that I am not allowed to have in my room: the green tray from the kitchen with the holes that I use to sort my gummy bears, the bag of makeup that Mom does not know is missing from her bathroom, and most importantly, my jump rope. Dad took away my jump rope the last time I used it in the house because I knocked over a lamp, but I found its hiding spot in the garage and brought it back inside. (It was not even very hard to find because Dad is no good at choosing hiding spots. He put it under my bicycle helmet on the bottom shelf of our storage cabinet. If I were hiding a jump rope, I would put it some-where that no one else could ever find it—or at least on the top shelf.)

I shimmy out from under my bed and try to tie the two ends of my jump rope together into a knot. I do not really like to tie knots, not even on my shoes, which is why I always ask for shoes with no laces. I weave one end of the rope around the other and pull tightly, and a knot forms in the middle, which is not where I wanted it. I try again, weaving the ends together twice this time before pulling it, and I make a knot right where I need it, turning the jump rope into an enormous circle.

I put the jump rope over my head and pull it down to my belly button. Then I twist it in the middle and try to pull it back over my head again, but it is too short and my nightgown gets tangled in it. I stomp my foot and tug the rope back over my head.

"I don't need you, rope," I say, throwing it down, and I march over to my bed and pick up a pillow. I flop my Rainbow Sparkle pillowcase up and down, holding the corners, just like I see Mom do when she changes the sheets. It takes a lot of work to get the pillow out, but when I do, I take the pillowcase and try to tie the corners together into a knot. Tying this is even harder than tying the jump rope, and I am running out of time.

I toss the pillowcase back on my bed and run over to my closet. I take out a pink zippy sweat-shirt, which I try never to wear because I hate pink. I place it on my bed, pull the sleeves up in the air, and tie them together at the wrists. Then I hang the sweatshirt over my shoulder like a hand-bag and put my right arm through the opening. It still doesn't feel right, so I pull the tied sleeves over my head and hang it on my left shoulder.

And then my sling is perfect!

It would be more perfect if it were covered in glitter and had a periwinkle cast inside, but it is still pretty great.

I am standing in front of my closet door, admiring my new sling in the mirror, when Dad barges into my room.

"Good morning, Man—" he starts to say, but then he stops short right past my doorway. I turn to see what he is looking at: the jump rope.

Oh no.

"How did this get in here?" he asks, and he walks over and scoops it into his hand, which I don't think is very nice.

"Why aren't you at work yet?" I ask. Mom always wakes me up for school, and she doesn't care about jump ropes being inside the way Dad does.

"Why do you have this jump rope in your room after I said it wasn't allowed?"

"I needed it for something," I tell him honestly.

"Is she up?" Mom appears in my doorway behind Dad.

"Oh, she is indeed . . . ," Dad answers her. "Give me a kiss before I leave, Mandy. And I'm taking this jump rope with me. To work this time."

I try to cross my arms to show that this is not fair, but my right arm is stuck in my sling. Dad kisses me on the forehead and walks out the door.

"Good luck with that," he mumbles to Mom on the way out, and she looks me up and down, squinting her eyes.

"What do you have going on there?" she asks, motioning to my sling. I whip it off my shoulder and over my head and try to untie the sleeves quickly.

"I think I will wear this today," I tell her. I cannot tell Mom the plan about the sling, but if I can bring this sweatshirt to school, I can remake it on the bus, before Mrs. Spangle sees that my arm is not really hurt.

"I think you will not," Mom tells me. "Your arm isn't broken. You don't need a sling."

"But—"

"No," Mom says flatly. "Now pick out something else that you want to wear today, or I'm picking for you. You have five minutes to get dressed. No funny business."

Mom takes the pink zippy sweatshirt out of my hands and turns to walk out the door.

"Plus," she calls over her shoulder, "I thought you hated pink."

At school Anya has to help Natalie put away her book bag, take out her pencil case, hand in her seatwork, check out a book from the library, and unpack her whole lunch box. She is so busy helping Natalie all morning that she barely says anything to me, and this is very much not okay. Especially because Mrs. Spangle is making me miss recess again today, so I cannot even talk to her then.

Kids who have to miss recess stand by themselves under a tree, which is no fun at all. I lean against the tree and watch Anya push Natalie on a swing, and I feel my face get hot from anger.

"Anya!" I call across the playground, but Anya doesn't hear me.

"ANYA!" I try again. Nothing.

"ANYA VALENTINA ZOLIN!" I yell her full name, and finally, Anya turns around. My voice is going to get worn out from all of this yelling if people do not start listening to me. I gesture for her to come over to my tree, and Anya shakes her head.

"COME HERE!" I yell.

"I can't!" Anya yells back. "I'll get in trouble!"

But Anya was never so worried about getting in trouble before she was Natalie's buddy. Natalie is allergic to trouble, and if I don't fix this problem soon, she is going to ruin Anya forever.

I am stuck here by this tree until recess is over, so the only way I can get Anya to come over to me is if I have to go inside to the nurse. The aides make you take a buddy with you when you leave the playground, so I can make Anya be mine. I look down at the ground, which is kind of sandy right under the tree. I reach my right hand down, and when my fingertips touch the sand, I lift up my left leg and try to fall forward. When nothing happens, I try to kick my right knee with my left foot to knock myself down.

Still standing.

I lift the top of my body back up again and try to fall down more quickly, but I only land on my hands and knees. I stand again and try to fall

sideways, but my right knee hits the ground first and ruins the rest of the fall. I walk three feet forward and drag my left toes over a tree root to trip, and I barely even stumble.

I am never going to get to the nurse if I cannot get a good scrape. And if I cannot go to the nurse, then I can't get Anya to be the one to walk me to her office.

I get down on my knees and try to slam my left elbow hard into the ground, but it only makes a hole in the sand. I jump up and down on my tippy toes, and I try to do a cartwheel, and I flop into a forward roll, and nothing, nothing, nothing. I walk five giant steps away from the tree and am just about to run straight into it when I hear a whistle from across the playground.

Tweet, the whistle blows again.

"Young lady," the lunch aide calls. "Young lady

by the tree." She is pointing right at me. "Whatever you're doing over there, knock it off."

I slump down with my back against the tree and cross my arms. I look down at myself and notice for the first time that there is dirt all over my clothes, scratches on my arms, and best of all, my knee is bleeding. Just a little tiny bit, but it is good enough.

I stand up and shoot onto my tippy toes and wave my hand in the air.

"Excuse me!" I call to the lunch aide. "EXCUSE ME!" I jump up and down in place until she turns around.

"What is it?" she answers me.

"I need to go to the nurse!" I call back. "I'm bleeding." And I can't be sure, because she is super far away, but I think the aide lets out an enormous sigh then.

"Fine," she calls back. "Take a buddy with

you." Before she can tell me not to, I dart onto the playground and over to the swings. I grab Anya by the arm and begin to pull her away from Natalie.

"Come on, you have to take me to the nurse," I tell her.

"What?" she says. "Why do you need to— why are you so dirty?"

"I fell down," I answer. "Now hurry."

Anya and I walk up the sidewalk back to the building.

"Do you think the nurse will have periwinkle Band-Aids?" I ask her.

"I don't know," Anya answers. "I hope so. Can we stop and get a drink at the water fountain first?" And this is why Anya is my favorite person in the world, at least most of the time. Because she knows how important periwinkle Band-Aids and trips to the water fountain are.

"You're my friend, right?" I ask her. "Not Natalie's."

"I'm Natalie's friend too," she answers, which is not what I wanted her to say.

"But me more," I say.

"Yes, you more," Anya tells me as we reach the fountain. She bends down to take a sip, and when she stands back up, water is dripping down her chin. I grab her wrist again and drag her with me to the nurse's office, and I hold on to her the whole time just to make sure that she cannot run away from me.

CHAPTER 5

Jungle Jam

IT IS A WHOLE DAY LATER, and Anya is still Natalie's buddy, so my life is pretty much ruined.

"You should not help her so much," I say to Anya when she opens Natalie's lunch box for her and unwraps her sandwich.

"She only has one arm, Mandy," Anya tells me, like I am some kind of dope or something. And I am pretty angry with Anya then, because she is not remembering that she is supposed to be *my* friend more than she is Natalie's.

Anya even laughed at something Natalie said during seatwork, which is just ridiculous, because Natalie never says anything funny. And when I leaned my chair back on two legs to ask what was so funny, they did not tell me, and then Mrs. Spangle put my initials on the board for rocking in my chair again.

When lunch is over, we line up for recess, and I do not stand near Anya because she is with Natalie. Instead, I end up stuck in front of Dennis, which is just awful. Dennis keeps pulling at the ends of my hair, and I tell him to stop, so he does it some more. I wish I could pull on his hair to show him how it feels, but his Mohawk is too short for me to tug.

Dennis is pretty terrible, if I forgot to mention.

"What are you going to do at recess, Polka Dot?" he asks me.

"None of your beeswax," I answer.

"Do you want to play TV tag?" Dennis asks. "Or are you too slow?" TV tag is Dennis's favorite game ever, because Dennis watches a lot of TV, so he is very good at not getting tagged. The only TV show I watch all the time is Rainbow Sparkle's, except when it is taken away as punishment, so I think TV tag is dumb.

"I do not play TV tag," I tell him. The lunch aides open the doors then, and we run out onto the playground. I see Anya and Natalie skip over to the monkey bars, which is silly because Natalie cannot even do the bars with her one stupid arm.

"Mandy!" Anya calls from across the playground. "Come play with us!" But I do not answer her because I am not going to play with Natalie. No way!

I walk around the playground by myself, which is pretty lonely, if I am being honest. But the swings are all taken and the slide is too hot and there is nothing for me to do unless I play TV tag with Dennis or swing on the monkey bars with Natalie, and I am not doing either.

I kick up sand as I wander around the edge of the playground, with no friends and nothing to do. I kick one rock and then another, trying to send them as far into the air as possible so that they crash down into the sand. Gray rock, black rock, white rock, copper rock . . .

Copper rock?

I lean my nose farther toward the ground and dig for the rock I just kicked. As sand fills my fingernails, I find it, and it's not a rock at all. It's a penny! I scoop the penny into my palm and blow the rest of the sand off it, and then I stick it in my pocket to keep it safe. I am not going to lose this coin like I lost the others. It is the only good thing to happen to me today. Maybe the only good thing all week.

"Hey, Polka Dot," Dennis calls to me. "How

come you're not playing with your twin?"

"What are you talking about, Freckle Face?" I ask.

"Anya," Dennis says. "Your twin. How come you're not playing with her on the monkey bars?"

"Because I do not want to," I answer.

"Because she's better at the monkey bars than you?" Dennis challenges.

"No way," I say. "I just do not want to."

"Liar," Dennis says. "There is no way you are better than her." He points to Anya, who is swinging across the bars two at a time, swiftly and smoothly, like a real monkey. "Anya is the best monkey barrer in second grade."

"She is not," I say. "I could totally beat her across the bars."

"No way," Dennis says.

"I bet you I can," I answer.

"Bet me what?"

I think about this for one second only, and then I dig into my pants pocket for the penny.

"This penny," I show him. "If Anya beats me across, I'll give you this penny. If I beat her, you'll give me a quarter."

"How is that fair?" Dennis asks. "If you beat her—which you won't—I'll give you another penny."

"Fine," I answer. "Let's go."

Dennis and I charge across the playground to the monkey bars. "Hey, Anya," he calls. "Polka Dot here wants to race you across the bars."

"Okay," Anya agrees with a shrug. She climbs back up the ladder and waits patiently, her hands draped over the first rung. I climb up next to her and place my own hands on the bar.

"I am going to beat you," I whisper-yell in her ear, and Anya shrugs again like she does not even care.

"Go Anya!" Natalie calls, and this makes me madder than ever.

"On your mark . . . ," Dennis counts down. "Get set . . . go!"

I swing myself off the ladder and grip the bar between my hands tightly. In less than a second Anya moves out ahead of me, one arm in front of the other, until she is halfway done with the bars, and I am still hanging on the first.

"Time out!" I call. "TIME OUT!" I hang still like a statue on the first bar, and Anya turns to me, her arms scissored out across three bars.

"What's the matter, Polka Dot?" Dennis asks. "Glued to the bar?"

"Anya got to practice first and I did not," I say. "She is all warmed up."

"That doesn't matter," Natalie pipes in. "Dennis only said that you wanted to—"

"Shut up, Natalie!" I interrupt her.

"Fine," Anya says. "I'll give you time to catch up to me, and we'll go from here."

"Fine," I agree. Anya stays hanging in the middle of the bars, and I drop my left hand and reach for the next one. I catch it with my fingertips and pull myself up, and then I force my right hand to follow. My hands scrape across the bar and it hurts a lot, but I am not going to give up.

"Oh, come on," Dennis calls. "This is not even a contest."

I release my left hand from the bar again and reach for the next one, but before I can grab it, my right hand slips off the bar and I fall to the ground with a thud. Anya lets go of the bars herself and rushes toward me.

"Are you okay?" she asks.

"NO!" I answer, and I stand and run away from the monkey bars as fast as I can, tears tickling the backs of my eyes.

I run all the way across the playground, and
then I crouch down and hide behind a tree. I
put my eyes against my knees and wrap my arms
around my legs. I hear footsteps running up

behind me, so I wipe the tear that has fallen on my cheek onto my pant leg.

"What's wrong?" Anya comes to a stop and stands over me.

"My hands hurt," I tell her. This is true—my hands do hurt from those dumb monkey bars, but they are not the real reason I am upset.

"Let me see," Anya says, so I hold out my hands to show her. "You don't have any blisters. They're just red."

"They hurt," I tell her.

"They'll feel better soon," Anya says. "My hands hurt, too, when I first started doing the monkey bars. I can help you practice if you want."

"No, thank you," I say. "Just go play with your best friend, Natalie."

"She's not my best friend," Anya tells me. "You are. I just have to be her buddy because her wrist is broken."

"I wish my wrist were broken," I tell her. "Then you could be my buddy instead of Natalie's."

"That's silly," Anya says. "I already am your buddy."

The lunch aide blows the whistle for us to line up, and Anya reaches out her hand to help me stand. I grab it, and she pulls me to my feet, and we walk off to join our class.

"But if I had a cast, you could be my buddy all the time," I explain. "Mrs. Spangle would have to let you sit next to me and take me to the bathroom and help me in the cubbies. Plus, I bet I would get fancy-dancy periwinkle sunglasses, because everyone would feel so sorry for me."

"You shouldn't break your arm to get sunglasses," Anya says. "That's dumb."

We reach our line, and she skips ahead to stand next to Natalie.

And I know then that Anya is right: I don't need to break my arm just to get fancy-dancy periwinkle sunglasses, but I do need to do something in order to get Anya back.

Something big.

CHAPTER 6

Jump, Jump, Splat!

THE TWINS ARE CRYING WHEN I GET HOME from school, which is not a shock because the twins are always crying.

"How was your day?" Mom asks as they wail, and I say, "Fine," even though it was not.

"I am going outside," I tell Mom. "Timmy is not allowed to come."

"Timmy is taking a nap," Mom says. "And no funny business today, do you hear me?"

"Yes," I answer, and I open the back door.

"Mandy," Mom calls behind me. "I mean it—you be on your best behavior out there."

"Okay," I answer, and I say the "kay" part super-duper loud, so Mom knows I heard her. I walk over to our swing set and sit on the swing farthest from the kitchen window. I pump my legs back and forth, and the swing rises in the air quickly. I may not be any good at the monkey bars, but I am an excellent swinger.

I pull my arms back and forth on the rope handles and move my body front and back at the same time as my legs. I swing as high as I can—so high that I could touch the moon if it were nighttime. I would jump off this swing right now, like the fourth graders do on the playground, except I do not know how to do that exactly.

I pump my legs back and forth very strongly, and push my body against the wind. I whizz through the air, my hair falling out of my ponytail and my nose so close to the clouds that I think I can smell them.

"What you doing, Mandy?" Timmy wanders out the back door and over toward the swing set.

"Why are you out here?" I ask. "I told Mom you were not allowed to come."

Timmy shrugs. "I wake up. What you doing?"

"Jumping off the swing," I tell him, even though I have not actually done that yet.

"I try too," Timmy says, and he pulls himself onto the swing next to me.

"You do not know how to jump off swings," I tell him. "You are a baby."

"I jump off steps," Timmy tells me.

"That is not even the same because—" I begin, but then I stop myself. I feel my eyes spread out wider and wider into humongous pancakes.

Because Timmy has just given me a great idea.

I hop off the swing and jog toward the back door.

"Where you going, Mandy?" Timmy calls after me, but I do not answer him. I do not have time to talk to preschoolers when I have finally found a way to make my week better in a big way. I run through the house until I am at the bottom of the steps, then I climb up the first one. I turn around, jump as high as I can in the air, and land on the ground.

On two feet.

So I turn and climb up two steps and jump high in the air again.

And I still land on two feet.

"What you doing, Mandy?" Timmy appears around the corner.

"Shh. Mom cannot hear."

"But what you doing?"

"Breaking my arm," I tell him. "Now shush,

because it is a secret." Timmy slides his hand across his mouth like it is a zipper, and he watches me as I climb all the way up to the third step. I turn around, take a deep breath, and leap toward the floor.

And my feet slip out from under me, and I land on my bottom. And my bottom kind of hurts.

But my arms do not.

"What was that crash?" Mom calls from some-where in the house, so I hurry back onto my feet and run up four steps before Mom finds out what I'm doing. I take a gigantic breath, turn around, and—

"AMANDA!"

—find Mom standing at the bottom of the steps.

"What did I tell you two about jumping off the steps?" she says.

"You did not tell me," I point out. "You told Timmy."

"Funny how you listen when I give Timmy directions," Mom says to me. "Is there a reason you don't when I tell you no funny business today?"

"Because you are not funny!" I yell, and I stomp my foot and cross my arms and begin to pound my way up the stairs to my room.

"Wait just a minute," Mom calls after me. "Come back down here right now, young lady."

I turn on my tippy toes without looking at Mom and bang my feet loudly on the way down. I think about jumping down the last three steps, but Mom is standing in my way.

"Would you like to tell me what you were doing?" she asks.

"No, thank you," I answer, and I am polite and everything.

"Timmy," Mom says, "can you tell me what Mandy was doing?"

"She was breaking her arm," Timmy answers. And he looks pretty proud of himself.

"Why were you trying to break your arm?" Mom squints her eyes into slits at me.

"So I can get Anya to be my buddy and not Natalie's," I answer.

"Listen to me carefully," Mom begins. "You are not to break your arm, or your leg, or your finger, or your nose, or anything. Do you understand me?"

I nod, but I still do not look at her.

"I thought practicing giving other people attention was helping, but I guess not," she says. "I guess I'm going to have to take away Rainbow Sparkle's TV show until you learn—"

"No!" I yell. "I don't even want attention. I just want Anya back."

Mom looks from my forehead to my toes like she doesn't believe me. "Did you and Anya have a fight?"

"No, but she is not acting like my best friend anymore," I tell her. "She is acting like Natalie's."

"Anya can be friends with both you and Natalie, you know," Mom says.

"I. Do. Not. Share. Anya." I say each word like it has its own period after it. "Anya is *mine*!" I stare right at Mom then, so that she knows I mean business. And I feel my own eyes tickling with tears again, but I rub my hands against the lids to push them back inside.

Mom looks at me for a couple of seconds without saying a word, then she reaches out her hand and takes one of my nonbroken wrists. Without pulling too hard, she leads me to the kitchen table, which is still covered in twin stuff. She sits me in a chair at the head of the table and puts herself in the one right next to me.

"Timmy, go to your room for a while," she says. "I need to talk to Mandy in private." And I like to talk to Mom with no Timmy and no twins around, so that is something, I guess.

Mom leans forward. "Tell me what's happening with Anya," she says.

"I did already." I cross my arms on my chest.

"Start at the beginning," Mom says.

So I sigh a big gust of breath and begin: "Natalie broke her stupid wrist—"

"No 'stupid' talk," Mom interrupts, which I do not think should be allowed.

"Natalie broke her wrist, and Mrs. Spangle made me her buddy. But Natalie is very bossy, so I did not want to be her buddy. And then Mrs. Spangle moved Natalie's seat away from me and made Anya her buddy. So now Anya spends all of her time with Natalie and not with me," I finish. "It is a tragedy."

Mom smiles a little bit at me then, which is not very nice. "Anya is just spending extra time with Natalie because she needs help right now. She's still your friend too."

I shake my head back and forth very quickly. "No, she plays with her on the playground. And she sits with her at lunch. And she laughs at Natalie's jokes, and Natalie is never funny." I take a big breath. "I think she likes Natalie better than me."

"Did you talk to Anya about it?"

"Yes, and she said I was being dumb," I say. "She doesn't listen to me. She only listens to Natalie."

"I'm sure that's not true," Mom says. "Try to talk to her again tomorrow—nicely. See what she says."

I shrug my shoulders up to my ears. "I don't feel like it."

"Friendship is hard work, Mandy," Mom says. "If you and Anya want to be friends—which I know you do—sometimes you have to do things that you don't want to. You can't just mope around and act like a crankypants and expect things to work out. Okay?"

"Okay," I answer quietly.

"Good." Mom nods with satisfaction. "And listen to me—I don't want to hear or see one more thing about broken bones. Do you understand me?"

I look at Mom's nose and do not answer.

"Mandy," she warns me, "I mean it. No broken bones in the Berr house. You are not to hurt yourself. Understood?"

"Yes," I say. "Does breaking a bone hurt?"

"Very, very much," Mom says. "I broke my ankle in middle school. Believe me—you don't want to do it."

"How'd you break it?" I ask, because the story is the best part of breaking a bone.

"I fell down the stairs at my friend's house," Mom answers. "Do you see now why I'm always telling you and your brother to stop jumping off the stairs? It's dangerous."

I nod, because I think Mom is forgetting to punish me, and that is great news.

"Now remember: No broken bones and no B-R-A-T behavior," Mom says, standing up from the table.

"Brat!" a voice calls from behind me, and I whip around to find Timmy sitting on the third step, not minding his own beeswax.

"Hey!" I leap from my chair. "We were supposed to be talking in private!" I run at my fastest speed ever toward the steps, and Timmy scrambles to get up them as fast as a preschooler can scramble. I start to chase him, and I am just about to grab the sock off his foot when Mom appears behind us.

"NO FUNNY BUSINESS ON THE STAIRS, YOU TWO!" Mom yells.

Timmy and I stand like statues for a moment, then I march past him up the steps and into my room without saying one word. I slam the door behind me and jump onto my bed, pulling my bag of gummy bears out from under my pillow. I pick out a green bear and bite off one of its arms, and I do not even give him a buddy to help him.

Because gummy bears never, ever need a stupid cast.

CHAPTER 7

Following the Leader

"I NEED TO TALK TO YOU," I SAY TO ANYA when we're both in the cubbies the next morning. "My mom said so."

"Okay," Anya answers. "What do you want to talk about?"

"Nat—" I begin, but before I can even finish her name, Natalie appears behind Anya's shoulder.

"Good morning, Anyie," she says, and Anya gives her a big smile—the kind of smile she is only supposed to give her best friend.

"Hi, Natty," Anya answers, and I feel my chin drop down so low that my tongue may be hanging out of my mouth.

"Absolutely not!" I yell, and Anya and Natalie both look at me with eyes as wide as pancakes. "No nicknames!"

"What's wrong, Polka Dot?" Dennis pipes in. "Lose another coin?"

"Shut up, Dennis!" I yell. "I am not talking to you."

"Hey, folks in the cubbies, wrap it up in there!" Mrs. Spangle calls from her desk. "You have seat-work waiting that isn't going to write itself."

"Anyie, can you help me with my sweater, please?" Natalie asks Anya, and I give her my meanest look ever.

"What did you want to talk to me about?" Anya asks me as she pulls a sleeve of Natalie's cardigan off her cast.

"Never mind." I turn around quickly and walk to my desk in a huff and a puff.

"Hey, Polka Dot," Dennis whispers behind my ear. "You still owe me that penny."

"Do not," I say.

"Do too," Dennis argues. "You lost the monkey bar race to Anya. That was the deal."

"I didn't lose," I say. "I did not even finish."

"Right," Dennis answers when I tell him this. "That means you lost."

I shake my head ferociously. "No, I didn't get to finish," I respond. "I was still practicing."

"Nope, lost," Dennis insists. "Loser."

I would ask Anya what she thinks, but she is too busy carrying Natalie's stuff to her desk and helping Natalie rip the correct page out of her math workbook and giving Natalie best friend nicknames. So I reach into my desk and give Dennis the penny that I was hiding in the

corner, because I do not feel like arguing about it anymore, and I always feel like arguing with Dennis. And now I have no coins again, so there is no way I am ever going to be able to buy my own fancy-dancy periwinkle sunglasses.

I place my elbows on my desk and rest my chin in my hands, and I do not even let out one "Wahoo!" when Mrs. Spangle tells us we are going to have fifteen minutes of extra recess this afternoon, even though I love recess.

"If you're finished with your seatwork, Mandy, you have time to do some silent reading," Mrs. Spangle calls from her desk. So I pull out my Rainbow Sparkle book, but I do not read it. Instead, I lay my head down on my arms and close my eyes.

And I am trying not to cry again, if I am being honest, because everything is awful.

I have no coins and no sunglasses and no best

friend, and I do not know how to do the monkey bars, which I didn't even know I couldn't do before. I squeeze my eyes shut and push the tears back inside with my pinkies, and I try to think about gummy bears and Rainbow Sparkle because they are the only things that still make me happy.

"Mandy," I hear Mrs. Spangle whisper from her desk. "Mandy."

I whip my head up and look at my teacher, and she is a little bit blurry behind the mist in my eyes. She wiggles her finger back and forth for me to approach her desk.

I wipe the backs of my hands across my eyes as I walk toward Mrs. Spangle, and I just know she is going to put my initials on the board again, and I do not even care why.

"Are you feeling okay?" Mrs. Spangle asks.

I nod my head, even though I am not. But I

am not really sick—I am just sick of Natalie and Dennis and my two working wrists.

"Are you sure?" Mrs. Spangle asks again. "You're not acting like yourself."

I nod again, because Mrs. Spangle will not understand my problems.

"Just having a bad day?" she asks.

"A bad week," I answer.

"Do you want to tell me about it?"

"No, thank you," I say, and I am polite and everything.

Mrs. Spangle smiles a little then, which I think is rude. She places her fingers under my chin and lifts it a tiny bit. "Buck up," she says. "You just keep plugging away, and I bet it gets better."

I nod again, and I am pretty sure I have never been so quiet in my life.

"Remember, the Mandy I know never gives

up," Mrs. Spangle tells me. "Even if she is having a bad week. Am I right?"

"You're right," I say, but I am not sure that I mean it.

Mrs. Spangle gives me a sad face that matches my own. "I hate to see you like this."

"My mom says I am a crankypants," I tell her, and Mrs. Spangle smiles.

"Well, what can I do to cheer you up?" she asks.

"Nothing," I answer, because I am absolutely positive that Mrs. Spangle will not know how to make Anya my best friend again instead of Natalie's.

"I have an idea," Mrs. Spangle tells me. "Julia is absent, and she is supposed to be our Line Leader this week. How about you take her place for the day? I know you like that job."

"Really?" I clap my hands together and then

shoot my fist in the air. "Wahoo!" Being the Line Leader is the best of all of the classroom jobs, because you get to be at the front of the line and be in charge, and best of all, Mrs. Spangle always holds the Line Leader's hand in the hallway. I got to be the Line Leader the third week of second grade, but I have a very long wait until Mrs. Spangle makes it all the way through the rest of my class and back to my name. I know this because when she switches the classroom jobs every Monday, I ask her if it is my turn to be Line Leader yet.

"There's the Mandy I know," Mrs. Spangle says. "Now skedaddle back to your seat and do some silent reading. We have two minutes before we go to special subject."

I bounce away from Mrs. Spangle's desk and back to my own. I lift my Rainbow Sparkle book off my desk and pretend to read it, but I am too jittery from Line Leader excitement to concentrate.

After what feels like many, many minutes, Mrs. Spangle announces that it is time to go to special subject, so I stuff my book back into my desk and sit up very straight with my hands folded, waiting.

"Look at the great example our Line Leader is setting," Mrs. Spangle tells the class, pointing at me. "Go ahead and start the line for us, Mandy."

I leap from my seat and push my chair in super fast, then I walk as quickly as I can to our classroom door.

"Hey, Polka Dot's not the Line Leader," Dennis calls out. "Julia is."

"Julia's absent today," Mrs. Spangle explains. "And what did I tell you about name-calling?" When Mrs. Spangle looks away, Dennis sticks his tongue out at me, but I am too busy focusing on being the Line Leader to care.

"Let's see which groups look like they're ready for special subject," Mrs. Spangle continues, and she tells them to get in line one by one—all behind me, because I am in charge. Dennis walks to the line the slowest, because he always likes to be the caboose.

"Okay, Mandy," Mrs. Spangle calls from her desk. "Get us going."

"Aren't you coming?" I call back.

"I'll catch up in a second," Mrs. Spangle says, moving around piles of papers on her desk. "You're in charge."

I take a deep breath and step into the hallway, looking over my shoulder to make sure everyone is following me. I make a left out of our classroom and take ten medium-size steps down the hall—not too big and not too small—so that everyone can keep up. I am an excellent Line Leader, I think.

I look behind me and grin super wide when

I see my whole class following me. I take ten more medium-size steps and then look back again to see what is taking Mrs. Spangle so long to come hold my hand. I see her in the middle of our line, and I stop at the corner near the library, just like I am supposed to, and wait for her to catch up to me.

"Mrs. Spangle!" I whisper-yell, but instead of coming to meet me, Mrs. Spangle only waves her arm to signal me to keep going. And that's when I see it: the reason Mrs. Spangle is not holding my hand.

She is holding Natalie's hand. The one that is not covered by the cast.

I am absolutely positive that I have never been so angry in my life.

I flip my face forward and begin walking much faster down the hallway, not caring anymore if my class can keep up. I reach the end of the library and do not even stop at the corner before making a right, and I march at full speed toward the art room.

"Mandy! Mandy!" I hear calls behind me, but I ignore them because you are not supposed to talk in the hallway, and also, I am too busy being angry.

"Mandy!" I recognize Mrs. Spangle's voice. I whip my head around to face her, even though I don't want to, and I see the rest of my class waiting at the other end of the hall. Mrs. Spangle points to the door they're standing near. "We have music today, not art."

I feel my forehead get hot, and Dennis starts laughing at me loudly.

"It's okay," Mrs. Spangle says. "We all make mistakes, Dennis." She shoos my class into the music room while I shuffle back down the hall with my head down. I take my place in line behind Dennis—even farther back than the caboose.

"You're not such a hot Line Leader," he says, and Anya does not even care enough to be here to stick up for me. I guess it is no wonder that Anya wants to be Natalie's friend and not mine. Because no one wants to be friends with a bad Line Leader.

CHAPTER 8

Bad Mood Berr

THE WORST PART ABOUT HAVING THE MOST AWFUL week of your life is that everyone keeps asking, "What's wrong, Mandy?" and I say, "Everything," and they think I am kidding. But I am not even joking one bit, because everything is horrible and it's all because of Natalie.

I do not like that Natalie has a cast and a broken wrist and a secret story about how she did it, and I do not like that I have no change to go to the magic coin machine and buy fancy-dancy periwinkle sunglasses, but they are not even my worst problems. The biggest problem is that Anya has not been my best friend all week, and that is a tragedy. And it is not just a little tragedy—it is the most gigantic tragedy ever in my life, except for maybe when the twins were born.

I thought we were best friends again during music, because Anya sat next to me on the carpet instead of next to Natalie, and I had never been so happy in my life. So when we were back in our classroom, I asked her, "Do you want to go on the swings at recess?" I wanted to make sure that she would play with me today and not with Natalie, but she didn't answer me.

"Psst, Anya." I looked over at Mrs. Spangle to make sure she was not watching, then I rocked my chair back on two legs until I was as close to Anya as I could get. "Do you want to go on the swings at recess?"

"Maybe," Anya whispered, and then she turned her face away from me and leaned over her paper.

By the time we get to lunch, I do not know if we are friends again or not. I slap my lunch box onto the cafeteria table next to hers and sigh my biggest sigh, and she only covers her ears and says, "You are being very loud." And this is just ridiculous, because Anya loves loud noises.

"You always slam your lunch box too," I tell her. "Remember?" And I pick up her lunch box myself to show her.

"Stop, Mandy!" she yells, and she grabs her lunch box away from me before I can slam it. "It's too loud."

"I agree," Natalie says, even though no one asked her. And I realize then why Anya hates loud noises now: Natalie. Natalie has ruined her.

Natalie ruins everything.

Anya does not speak to me all through lunch,

but I do not speak to her, either, because I have never been so angry in my life. Instead, I watch Anya punch the straw into Natalie's juice box and untwist the lid on Natalie's thermos and be Natalie's friend instead of mine.

As we walk outside for recess, Dennis asks Anya, "Aren't you going to have a rematch with Polka Dot on the monkey bars soon? So you can beat her all over again?"

Anya shakes her head. "No, I don't feel like it," she says. And I am happy that I do not have to do the monkey bars again, but I am not happy when I see Anya and Natalie walk off to the side of the playground to sit in the sand together. I run after them and stand behind Anya's shoulder.

"I thought we were going to swing," I tell her.

"We're playing tic-tac-toe," Natalie answers, and I see Anya dragging a stick through the sand to draw the board.

"I was not talking to you," I say. "*Anya*, I thought we were going to swing."

Anya shakes her head again. "I don't feel like it," she says. "I just want to be quiet." Without another word, she draws an *X* in the middle square of the board, and then she draws an *O* in the corner where Natalie points her finger.

Anya is pretty much playing tic-tac-toe by herself, since Natalie cannot draw in the sand with her left hand, and the game looks even more dull than usual.

"It would be much more fun to play with me," I tell Anya.

"Tic-tac-toe is only for two people," she answers rudely. I feel my eyes widen into pancakes then, because I am absolutely positive that this is the meanest thing Anya has ever said to me.

"I meant it would be more fun to play with me *on the swings*," I say, and then I turn on my heels and run away from them. I run far across the playground and lean against a tree, and I am surprised that my eyes do not feel ticklish from tears. But I am not sad, I think—I am mad. Super-duper mad. More mad than I have ever been in my life.

And I am not just mad at Natalie; I am mad at Anya, too. I decide I am going to make a new best friend and show Anya what it is like to lose her favorite person in the world. I am going to eat lunch with my new friend and go on the swings with my new friend and tell Anya that there is only room for my new friend and me to play tic-tac-toe.

The only problem is that I don't really feel like making friends right now, and plus, I only know how to be friends with Anya.

Dennis runs up to me and asks me to play TV tag, and I say, "Yes," even though I do not want to.

He tags me and yells, "You're it," and I run after him across the playground very slowly.

"Hey!" he turns and calls back to me, his Mohawk blowing a little bit in the wind. "You're not even trying!"

And I stop running and shrug because Dennis is right. I turn around and walk away until I reach the swings, but when I sit on one, I do not even try to fly to the moon.

"Hey, Polka Dot," Dennis says. "What's wrong?"

"Everything," I answer, and Dennis rolls his eyes up to the sky, which I think is rude, even for Dennis.

"Come on, Polka Dot," Dennis begs. "I'll be 'it' this time, if you want."

"No, thank you," I say. And I do not call Dennis "Freckle Face" or tell him that my underwear is not even polka dot today, because I do not care about Dennis right now.

"Suit yourself," he says, and he runs away across the playground. So I spend the whole rest of recess on the swing by myself, without a single friend in the whole entire universe.

* * *

When I get home from school, Mom asks, "What's wrong, Mandy?" and I say, "Everything."

"That can't be true," she says. "Tell me what happened."

"Natalie happened," I explain. "Natalie and her stupid broken wrist."

"What did I tell you about this broken bone talk?" Mom says. "No broken bones in the Berr house."

I shake my head back and forth quickly because Mom does not understand. "That is not the problem," I tell her.

"Then what is?" Mom asks.

"Anya is not my friend anymore. Not even a little bit," I say real quiet-like.

"What? I can't hear you."

"Anya is not my friend anymore," I repeat, but a twin starts crying then, and I do not want to say it any louder.

"Anya? I thought you two talked and worked things out."

"No, she is Natalie's best friend now," I tell her.

"She's what? Wait, I still can't—hold on," Mom says, and she scoops the crying twin into her arms just as the other one starts wailing. "I'll be back to you in one second."

But I know it will take many more seconds to make those twins stop crying, so I escape from Mom because I do not want her to call me a "crankypants" again anyway. I tiptoe up the stairs to my room, twist the doorknob all the way to the right, and close it behind me as quietly as I can so no one can hear me turn the lock. Then I flop onto my bed and lie on my stomach with my chin in my hands and stare out the window. It is a cloudy day, which is perfect, because I am in a cloudy mood. And plus, I do not have any sunglasses.

CHAPTER 9

Bathroom Buddies

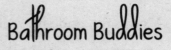

BY MONDAY MORNING I AM JUST AS MAD at Anya as I was at school on Friday. Actually, I am even more mad, because Anya could have at least called me after our fight and said, "I am sorry for being a crummy best friend, Mandy," but she did not. Not all weekend. And I did not call her either, because I am right and she is wrong.

There is absolutely, positively no way I want to see Anya at school today, so I wake up with a nervous and jumpy feeling. I slide my whole body underneath the covers and rub my palms up and down across my cheeks ferociously, then back and forth across my forehead. I sniff in as far as my breath will go until my nose feels stuffy. And then I wait.

"Mandy," Mom calls from the hallway, and I pop my head out from under the comforter as she opens my bedroom door. "Rise and shine, sleepy-head."

I twist my neck to the side of my pillow and try to look very weak.

"I'm sick," I tell her, and I try to make it sound like I have cotton balls in my throat. "I cannot go to school." I sniff all the way into my nose again, just so she knows I mean it.

Mom comes over to my bed and places the back of her hand on my forehead, and I know my face must be red and hot from rubbing it under the covers.

"Oh yeah?" Mom asks. "What hurts?"

"My head," I answer. "And also my nose."

"Your nose hurts?"

"It's stuffed up," I explain, and I sniff way up into my nostrils one more time.

"Hmm," Mom begins. "This sickness wouldn't have anything to do with your fight with Anya last week, would it?"

"No!" I say, and I sit up straight in bed before I remember. I lower myself back onto my pillow slowly, trying to look ill.

"Do you want to tell me more about what happened with Anya?" Mom asks. "You never explained the whole story."

"No," I answer. "I am too sick."

"Well, I'll take your temperature," Mom says. "But if it's normal, you're going to school."

"Fine," I answer, and as Mom goes to get the thermometer, I wonder if I can run to the bathroom and swallow some burning water to make my mouth super hot, but I do not have time. Mom comes back, sticks the cold, glassy end of the thermometer in my mouth, and we both wait.

"Whatever happened, I bet you and Anya will be fine today, anyway," Mom says. "You two can never stay mad at each other for long."

"Nopth yiss shime," I try to say with the thermometer hanging out of the corner of my lips.

"Shh," Mom says. "No talking with that in your mouth." And I do not think it is fair for Mom to talk to me when I cannot even answer, especially when I know that Anya and I are done being friends for good.

When the time is up, Mom pulls the thermometer out of my mouth and glances at it. "Ninety-eight point six," she announces. "Up and at 'em for school." She pats me on the knee and stands up from my bed.

"But my nose—" I begin to protest.

"Mandy," Mom says, with a warning in her voice, "no more stalling. I mean it. Get ready for school." And then I feel like a crankypants all over again.

I walk into my classroom on my tippy toes and try not to look in the direction of Anya's desk. I sit in my chair and do not even rock it on two legs, and I work on my seatwork quietly as Mrs. Spangle takes attendance.

"Natalie," she calls.

"Here."

"Mandy."

"Here."

"Dennis."

"Present."

"Anya."

Silence.

"Anya's out today?" Mrs. Spangle looks up from her list, and I am more surprised than anyone. Natalie shoots her left hand in the air.

"Yes, Natalie?" Mrs. Spangle calls on her.

"Who is going to be my buddy?" she asks, and she sounds pretty panicked actually.

"Everyone will help you out today, when you need it," Mrs. Spangle answers, and Natalie shoots her hand in the air again.

"Yes?" Mrs. Spangle calls on her.

"Can I come up to your desk?" Natalie asks. Mrs. Spangle nods, and Natalie trots over to her and whispers something in her ear. Mrs. Spangle glances around the room until her eyes land on me.

"Mandy, can you come here, please?" I slump my shoulders as I rise slowly to my feet.

Of course Natalie is getting me in trouble. I don't even know what I could have done to her, but it doesn't matter. Because Natalie is ruining my life.

But when I reach Mrs. Spangle's desk, all she asks me is: "Could you accompany Natalie to the bathroom?"

I nod, even though I do not want to, because at least I am not in trouble. Natalie and I head toward our classroom door.

"Thank you," Natalie whispers when we reach the hallway, and I am surprised she is being polite.

"Why do you need help in the bathroom?" I ask.

"You'll see," Natalie says. And when we get there, Natalie goes into one stall and tells me to go in the one next to her.

"Could you hand me some toilet paper, please?" she asks. "I can't unroll it."

I pull a huge glob of toilet paper from the

holder, climb onto the toilet seat carefully, and toss it over the side of my stall and into Natalie's.

"Arghh!" I hear from the other side of the wall, followed by a sound I almost never hear from Natalie's lips: laughing.

Natalie is not a very giggly person at all, so I am very surprised by this.

"Why are you laughing?" I ask.

"I'm covered in toilet paper," Natalie answers, and she snorts through her nose a little because she is laughing so hard. "Can you hand me some more? Most of this fell in the toilet. You can give it to me under—"

But before Natalie can finish, I tear off an even bigger mound of toilet paper, hop up onto the seat, and throw it over the side of my stall.

"Arghh!" Natalie screams again, and then she begins laughing even harder.

And I kind of like to make Natalie laugh, if I

am being honest, because it is usually very hard to do.

"No more, no more!" Natalie calls, but she is still laughing. "I meant you could just hand it under the wall and I would reach for it—arghh!"

I toss the biggest ball of toilet paper yet into the next stall. Natalie flushes the toilet and swings open her door, so I open mine, too. The floor of Natalie's stall is covered in ribbons of toilet paper, and her face is pink from laughing.

"I hope you used some of that," I say.

Natalie nods. "I caught a couple of pieces before they landed on the floor. Could you help me wash my hand now? I can't get my cast wet."

I begin to turn on the sink faucet, but Natalie stops me. "Mandy," she says, "my cast really can't get wet. I mean it."

"Don't worry, it won't," I tell her. I squirt a small drop of soap onto Natalie's left hand, and when she is finished rinsing, I help her dry it off with a paper towel. I am very careful and Natalie is too.

"See—all dry!" I say when we have finished.

"Thank you for helping me," she says.

"That was harder than I thought," I tell her, and Natalie nods.

"It's a big pain," she says. "The cast can't get wet, and it makes my arm itch, and I can't do anything with it. I can't wait until it comes off."

"Really?" I ask. "Because if I had a cast, I'd want to keep it on forever."

Natalie shakes her head back and forth quickly. "You would hate it after one day," she tells me. "Maybe even before. Plus, I can't do the monkey bars now."

"You know how to do the monkey bars?" I ask. "I am not so good at them." And I look down at the bathroom floor then, because monkey bar talk makes me think of Anya, and that makes me sad.

"I can teach you," Natalie says. "When my wrist is better. Then you can have a rematch with Anya and beat her."

"Why would you want me to beat Anya?" I ask.

Natalie shrugs. "She's kind of bossy," she tells me, and this makes me laugh so loudly that Natalie rises onto her tippy toes. "Please don't tell her I said that."

"I won't," I promise. "*If* you finally tell me how you broke your wrist."

Natalie sighs. "Do I have to?"

"I did just take you to the bathroom." I hold my nose and make my stinkiest face to show her what a big deal this is.

Natalie sighs again. "Do you promise not to tell anyone?"

I reach out my hand to pinky swear, and Natalie does the same with her good hand.

"I fell down in the bathtub," she tells me, and I wait quietly for the rest of the story. When Natalie only stares at me, my mouth drops open wide.

"That's it?" I ask. "That's what you're so embarrassed about?"

"I didn't have any clothes on," Natalie says very seriously. "My mom had to help me get dressed before I could go to the hospital."

"So?" I ask. "No one wears clothes in the bathtub. It would be more embarrassing if you *were* wearing clothes." And this makes Natalie laugh again, and I like to see her laugh face-to-face, because her eyes get crinkly like Grandmom's.

"I guess you're right," Natalie says. "Thanks again for your help."

"No problem," I say. "At least I know now that

I don't really want a cast after all, if it's that much of a pain."

Natalie nods. "My mom says to be careful what you wish for," she tells me. "So don't wish for this." She points to her cast. We walk back to our classroom side by side.

And Anya is still not there.

CHAPTER 10

Broken Bones

ANYA IS NOT AT SCHOOL THE NEXT DAY either, and Mrs. Spangle says that she is sick. I shoot my hand into the air.

"Yes, Mandy?" Mrs. Spangle calls on me.

"Is she real sick or fake sick?" I ask.

"What do you mean?"

"Is she sneezing and coughing and burning up, or is she just pretending?" I explain, and Mrs. Spangle crosses her arms on her chest like she thinks I am playing a joke on her.

"Why would Anya be pretending to be sick?" she asks me, and I shrug my shoulders then, because I guess grown-ups do not know about being fake sick. After all, I was almost fake sick just yesterday. Maybe Anya is upset about our fight too, only her mom believes her when she makes her face red and hot.

I rock my chair back on two legs and whisper in Natalie's ear, "Do you think Anya's really sick?" and Natalie nods her head.

"How do you know?" I whisper. I have been Natalie's buddy ever since yesterday, and we are still getting along, believe it or not.

"I don't think she would pretend," Natalie whispers back.

"Natalie!" Mrs. Spangle yells, and I am so startled by the sound of Natalie's name being said in a loud voice that I bang the front half of my chair down in a crash.

"And Mandy, too," Mrs. Spangle says. Without another word, she turns her back to us and writes both of our initials on the board. And I am pretty shocked.

Because Natalie has never, ever gotten her initials on the board before.

I turn around without raising my chair legs to see if Natalie is crying, but she doesn't look upset at all. Maybe Natalie is really not so boring.

Maybe that cast cured her allergy to trouble.

Grandmom is sitting at the kitchen table with Mom when I get home from school, and they are both holding a twin. Timmy is under the table in between their feet, playing with his action figures, which I think is dumb because action figures are boy toys (but, to tell you the truth, I would kind of like to play with them by myself sometimes).

"Mandy!" Grandmom greets me. "Come give

me some sugar." I walk up and kiss her, and I make sure not to let my lips get anywhere near the twin, because then they would be damp.

"How was your day?" Mom asks.

"Anya is still absent," I reply. "Mrs. Spangle says she's sick."

"Oh no," Mom says. "Do you want to call and check on her?"

I shake my head. "We are not talking, remember?" I explain.

"I think you should try anyway," Mom says. "Do you want me to call first and talk to her mom?"

I consider this for a moment and then nod. Mom stands up and fetches the kitchen phone. "What's Anya's number?" she asks, and I tell her, because I am very good at remembering it. Mom dials, and then I hear her speaking to Anya's mom. Before I know it, Mom is holding out the phone to me.

"Someone wants to talk to you," she says.

"Anya's mom wants to talk to me?"

Mom gestures for me to take the phone, and I hold it up to my ear. "Hello?"

"Hi, Mandy," comes a voice at the other end, and it is raspy and froglike.

"Who is this?" I ask.

"It's me, Anya."

"What happened to your voice?"

"I'm sick," Anya says. "Didn't Mrs. Spangle tell you?"

"I thought you were faking," I say.

"No."

"What's wrong with you?" I ask.

"Everything," Anya answers, and she sounds just like me for a second. "But I'm glad you called because . . ."

"Yes?"

"I'm sorry I was mean to you before," Anya

says in her frog voice. "I didn't feel good, and I know I wasn't nice."

"No, you were not," I agree. "You said you didn't like being loud. Remember?"

"I know. Everything sounded really loud to me because my head hurt. But you know I still like to be loud too," Anya tells me, and this is just about the best news I have ever heard.

"Don't worry. We are friends again now, right? So it is not a tragedy," I say.

"Right," Anya answers. "How is school?"

And I can't believe that it has taken me so long to tell Anya the big news. "Guess who got her initials on the board today?"

"Who?"

"Natalie!"

"No way!"

"I know," I say. "And also, she told me how she broke her arm, but she said I cannot tell anyone, even though it is not even embarrass-ing." And I do not say one peep about Natalie calling Anya bossy, because I promised I would not.

"Not even me?" Anya asks.

"I'm sure she'll tell you when you're back at school. It will give you something to look forward to," I say. "Plus, she said that when her wrist is bet-ter, she's going to help me learn to do the monkey bars. So we can have a rematch."

Anya is quiet for a second. "Is Natalie your new best friend or something?"

"What? No!" I yell. "You are my best friend."

"Good," Anya answers, and she sighs like she was holding her breath this whole time. "You're mine, too."

"Good." I nod with satisfaction.

"Listen, I'm going to go," Anya says. "All this talking is making my throat hurt."

"Okay, bye," I say, about to hang up. "Wait! Anya?"

"Yeah?"

"I'm glad we're best friends again," I tell her.

"Me too," she croaks out in her frog voice. "Bye."

I hang up the phone and turn to see Mom and Grandmom smiling at me. "Feel better?" Grandmom asks.

"Me or Anya?"

"Both," she answers.

"Yes." I nod ferociously. "Both."

"Good," Mom says. "Did you see these new bibs that Grandmom bought for the twins?" She points to the one hanging around a twin's neck, and it already has drool down the front. "Aren't they adorable?"

"How come *they* got a present?" I ask, but before anyone can answer, I hear a loud crinkling coming from under the kitchen table, and I bend over to see Timmy digging through a bag of gummy bears. Gummy bears! My gummy bears!

"Hey!" I yell. "Where did you get those?"

"Grandmom," Timmy answers with a mouth full of bears.

"I got a big bag for you and Timmy to share," Grandmom explains, and I am pretty sure that I have never been so angry in my life.

"I! Do! Not! Share! Gummy! Bears!" I say each word like there is an exclamation point after it. "I have to share everything—my house and my mom and my dad and my best friend and my coins and my swing set—and I will not share my gummy bears with Timmy!" I stomp my right foot on the ground and kick my left one into the bottom of the cabinets.

And for a second I am pretty sure I am going to faint.

"YOW!" I scream, and grab my foot. My eyes are instantly swimming in tears, and I think that my foot is going to fall off.

"Mandy, oh my goodness." Mom scrambles to give the second twin to Grandmom, and she lifts me onto the counter. She grabs a bag of corn out of the freezer, and I cannot believe she is going to cook dinner when I am about to lose a foot.

"Why would you do something like that?" she asks as she places the bag of corn around my toes. "What part of your foot hurts?"

"Everything," I answer. "But mostly this toe." I point to the long one right next to my big toe.

"Hold this bag around your foot for a while," Mom says. "I'm going to call the doctor. I hope you didn't break a bone."

"Noooo!" I moan. "I don't want a cast! Natalie said it is awful."

"Shh, I need to hear the doctor," Mom says. "It will be okay—don't worry." She kisses my forehead and turns away from me, so I sit on the counter whimpering with the corn wrapped around my toes, and I wish as hard as I can that I do not have to get a big clumpy cast, which would be horrible at going to the bathroom. Timmy quietly walks over to where I'm sitting and holds up his hand to me. I reach down, and he places a gigantic mound of gummy bears in my palm.

And my foot stops hurting for that second only.

Dad rushes home from work and takes me straight to the doctor, and the doctor tells me some good news and some bad news. The bad news is that I broke my toe. The good news is that I do not have to get a cast—he just wraps some thick white tape around my toes to hold them together. And Mom has to change the tape every day, so it will not get itchy and my foot can get wet and I will not need help going to the bathroom.

Plus, I can get a different person to autograph my tape every day if I want, and I have a good story to tell my class about what happened, and those are the best parts of having a broken bone anyway.

I show my foot to Mom and Grandmom when I get home, and they do not look as happy about it as I do.

"You know why this happened, Mandy?" Mom asks.

"I was being a B-R-A-T?" I answer.

"Bingo," Mom says. "No more bratty behavior. Eight years old is much too old for that."

I nod because I am not a baby, so I agree.

"Plus, you didn't even let me show you the present I got for you before getting so mad over the gummy bears," Grandmom says.

"What is it?" I ask, and I am excited all over again.

Grandmom reaches into her handbag and pulls out a pair of white sunglasses. "Here," she says. "Your very own pair of cat-eye fancy-schmancy—what do you call them?"

"Fancy-dancy sunglasses!" I fill in, and I drop the "periwinkle" part because these glasses are white. Normally I hate white things, but these sunglasses are so amazing that it does not even matter. Plus, I do not want to act like a B-R-A-T again.

"I love them!" I yell. I stick the glasses directly on my nose and throw my arms around Grand-mom's neck. "Thank you!"

"You're welcome," Grandmom answers. "Now,

make sure you don't stub any more of those precious toes." She points to my feet.

"I won't," I tell her. "Ooh, I forgot." I pull a penny out of my pants pocket. "I found this in the doctor's parking lot. Here." I hand it to Grandmom. "You can add it to your collection for the magic coin machine."

"I have an even better idea," Grandmom says, and she holds the penny between two of her fingers. "You know the other thing that coins are good for besides making dollars?"

"What?"

"Making wishes," Grandmom tells me. "Every time I find a coin on the ground, I make a wish."

"Really?" I ask.

"Yep," Grandmom answers. "Just be careful what you wish for."

"That's what Natalie told me," I tell her. "About getting a cast."

"So are you ready to make a wish on this penny?" Grandmom asks.

"Yes," I say, and Grandmom throws the coin on the floor so I can pick it up again. As I do, I make a wish in my mind, and it is not for a cast or for fancy-dancy periwinkle sunglasses or for a lifetime supply of my very own pizzas.

When I finish, Mom, Dad, and Grandmom are all looking at me like they are waiting for me to say something. "I can't tell you what it is, or else my wish won't come true," I explain.

"So what are you going to do with that penny?" Dad asks.

I think for one moment only. "I'm going to turn my piggy bank into a wishing bank," I say.

"You're not going to save up your change for the magic coin machine?" Mom asks.

"Nope," I answer. "Because you know what?"

"What?" Grandmom asks.

"Wishes are more magical than dollars anyway." I stick my new fancy-dancy sunglasses on my nose, hold the penny tightly in my hand, and begin to limp toward the stairs so I can place the coin in my wishing bank.

And in my head I wish for my toe to get better real quick, so I can finally learn to do the monkey bars as fast as Anya.

But don't tell anyone, please, or else my wish won't come true.

Mandy's Lessons:

1. EATING THE POINTS OFF ALL THE PIZZA SLICES IS NOT ALLOWED.
2. A CAST IS THE PERFECT ACCESSORY.
3. LEFT HANDS ARE NO GOOD AT GIVING AUTOGRAPHS.
4. IT IS NOT EASY TO FALL DOWN IF YOU TRY TOO HARD.
5. ONLY MONKEYS ARE GOOD AT THE MONKEY BARS.
6. FUNNY BUSINESS IS NOT ALWAYS FUNNY.
7. LINE LEADERS NEED TO KNOW WHERE THEY'RE GOING.
8. YOUR BEST FRIEND SHOULDN'T MAKE YOU A CRANKYPANTS.
9. CASTS ARE NOT GOOD AT GOING TO THE BATHROOM.
10. DON'T WISH FOR A BROKEN BONE JUST BECAUSE YOU WANT A CAST.

DON'T MISS MANDY'S FIRST ADVENTURE,

Don't Wear Polka-Dot Underwear
(AND OTHER LESSONS I'VE LEARNED)!

I KEEP TELLING MOM ABOUT THE WHITE PANTS, and she says to wear them anyway.

"They will make me fall down," I explain.

"Pants do not make you fall down, Amanda," Mom answers, because she does not understand anything at all.

"Yes, they do." I stomp my foot and cross my arms and put on my very best "I am pouting now" face. "White pants like dirt, and they will make me fall in it."

"Then be extra careful at recess, please," Mom says, holding the awful pants open for me to step in.

"No."

Mom sighs a big gust of breath in my face and stares at me with her "I mean business" eyes. "Amanda Berr, I am going to count to three."

"I will get ketchup on them," I say.

"One . . ."

"I will drop marker on them," I say.

"Two . . ."

I groan like a dinosaur and lift up one leg just so Mom will stop counting.

"Here is a deal," I begin. "I will wear these awful white pants if you buy me periwinkle pants." My favorite color is periwinkle. It is more beautiful than blue and more perfect than purple and it is a fun name to say. But I do not have one piece of periwinkle clothing, and I think this is

unfair. I checked my whole entire closet—shirts and shorts and dresses and ugly fancy blouses that Mom keeps in plastic until Easter. No periwinkle. I had held my periwinkle crayon from my box of 152 colors up to each piece, just to be sure. And still nothing.

"I'll look for some," Mom says, shaking the white pants in front of me.

"Today," I insist. "I want periwinkle pants today."

"I cannot get you periwinkle pants today," Mom says. "Why can't you just like a nice, normal color—like pink? How about if I get you pink pants?"

"I hate pink."

"Good, *these* pants aren't pink." Mom shakes the pants even more ferociously.

I grab the pants in my own two hands then. "I will dress myself. I am not a baby," I say.

"Fine," Mom answers. "Be downstairs and dressed in five minutes, Amanda. And in *those* pants. I don't have time for any more funny business today."

So I stuff my legs into the pants and stomp down to the kitchen table, and Mom does not even say, *Thank you for wearing the awful white pants, Mandy.*

Did you **LOVE** this book?

Want to get access to great books for **FREE?**